Anthony Pasquin

The Pin-basket to the Children of Thespis

A satire

Anthony Pasquin

The Pin-basket to the Children of Thespis
A satire

ISBN/EAN: 9783337820343

Printed in Europe, USA, Canada, Australia, Japan

Cover: Foto ©Andreas Hilbeck / pixelio.de

More available books at **www.hansebooks.com**

THE

PIN BASKET

TO

THE CHILDREN OF THESPIS.

A SATIRE.

WITH NOTES.

[Entered at Stationers'-Hall.]

THE Author designed to have published the PIN BASKET previous to the Opening of Drury-Lane Theatre, but was unavoidably prevented. The Delay, owing to the Nature of the Poem, has produced one or two very trifling Errors, which may be easily perceived and rectified as perused.

THE
PIN BASKET.

TO
THE CHILDREN OF THESPIS.

A SATIRE.

BY ANTHONY PASQUIN, A.

WITH NOTES BIOGRAPHICAL, CRITICAL, AND EXPLANATORY.

INVOLVING

His R. H. the DUKE OF CLARENCE.
MARGRAVE of ANSPACH.
DUKE of MARLBOROUGH.
DUKE of QUEENSBERRY.
DUKE of LEEDS.
The late LORD BARRYMORE.
LORD MULGRAVE.
LORD DERBY.
LORD MOUNTMORRES.
RIGHT HON. W. PITT.
RIGHT HON. H. DUNDAS.
RIGHT HON. E. BURKE.
RIGHT HON. C. J. FOX.
MARGRAVINE of ANSPACH.
LADY BUCKINGHAMSHIRE.
LADY LADE.
GENERAL TARLETON.
SIR JOHN LADE.
HON. MR ST. JOHN.
COLONEL HANGER.
Dr. DARWIN.
Dr. REES.
Dr. AIKIN.
Dr. THOMPSON.
Dr. NORBURY.
Dr. DAVIS.
Dr. TOWERS.
Dr. PARR.
Dr. ARNOLD.
Dr. WOLCOTT.
Mrs. ROBINSON.

Mrs. JORDAN.
Mrs. SIDDONS.
Miss FARREN.
Miss LEAKE.
Miss POPE.
Miss WALLACE.
Mrs. SERRES.
Signora STORACE.
Mrs. CROUCH.
Mrs. WELLS.
Mrs. POPE.
Mrs. BLAND.
Mrs. MATTOCKS.
Mr. SHERIDAN.
Mr. COLMAN.
Mr. CUMBERLAND.
Mr. M. A. TAYLOR.
Mr. RICHARDSON.
Mr. REYNOLDS.
Mr. BOADEN.
Mr. O'KEEFE.
Mr. GRUBB.
Mr. MORTON.
Mr. DUDLEY.
Mr. HOARE.
Mr. HOLCROFT.
Mr. COBB.
Mr. M. P. ANDREWS.
Mr. J. TAYLOR.
Mr. HARRIS.
Mr. WALTER.
Mr. LITCHFIELD.
Mr. NARES.

Mr. BELOE.
Mr. GODWIN.
Mr. CHALMERS.
Mr. PINKERTON.
Mr. BELSHAM.
Mr. MACKLIN.
Mr. BREWER.
Parson ROSE.
Parson ESTE.
Parson ARMSTRONG.
Mr. T. BYRNE.
Mr. DALMEYDA.
Mr. M'DONNEL.
Mr. BOURNE.
Mr. BARR.
Mr. MADDISON.
Mr. SHAW.
QUICK.
HOLMAN.
LEWIS.
BENSLEY.
PALMER.
DIGNUM.
KEMBLE.
SUETT.
KING.
BANNISTER.
SEDGWICK.
KELLY.
INCLEDON.
BRAHAM.
WALDRON.
Black DAVIS, &c. &c. &c.

DEDICATED
TO THE COUNTESS OF JERSEY.

LONDON:

PRINTED FOR THE AUTHOR;
AND SOLD BY J. S. JORDAN, FLEET-STREET.
1796.
(Price Three Shillings.)

TO THE COUNTESS OF JERSEY.

M ADAM,

Unlike the multitude of Dedicators, I shall be honest and inge-
nuous enough to confefs to your Ladyship, and the public, the real spur
that impelled me to make you the object of this Dedication. Men
select not satire in general as a vehicle of eulogy and flattery, but as an
engine whereby they may expose the vices and follies of mankind.—
This should be in the recollection of readers, and the author's merit, should
be confequently esteemed. My work will shew that I have been, for the most
part, particularly obfervant of fingling out characters *deferving* strains of
a very oppofite burthen to thofe of praife and commendation. The world
shall alfo exculpate me from any intention to make this the means of
forcing upon your Ladyship a draught, which, though fweet to fome as
mountain-thyme to bees,

וּמְתוּקִים מִדְּבַשׁ

וְנֹפֶת צוּפִים׃

would be *to you* both *naufeous* and *impertinent.* To come then immediately and truly to the point—A dedication was wanted to occupy a
page, and next, of courfe, fome name to complete that dedication. The
Archbifhop of Canterbury firft occurred to me as a very proper fubject,
and I had nearly determined to commit my *horde* into his *faving hands,*
when your Ladyship's name flafhed on my imagination, as promifing to

B

be more advantageous to my purpofe, therefore, although the poem had even lefs affinity to you, than to the *Archbifhop of Canterbury himfelf*, I decided in your favour.

To your Ladyfhip, then, I dedicate the following fheets ; and whatever obligation or honour you may think conferred on you, I beg you will afcribe it all, not to any veneration I have for your *unfpeakable* virtues, but more truly to the notoriety your Ladyfhip's name has lately *enjoyed;* and which alone, I have no doubt, will procure a fale to many of my *bafkets.*

In which fervent hope

I am, *(and fhould it be realized)*

With *due* gratitude,

Your Ladyfhip's

Moft obedient, very humble Servant,

Anthony Pasquin.

N O T E.

'Ουδὲν Θαυμαςὸν Πολυπαίδη· ἢ δὲ γὰρ ὁ Ζεὺς
'Ουϑ᾽ ὕων πάντας ἀνδάνει, ἐδ᾽ ἀνέχων.

THEOC.

NOT even the works of the Omnifcient Power are approved of all men; there are

" Who ever find occafion to complain."

And is it then for me to murmur, or you my friends to be furprifed, that fome fhould load me with diffenfious outcries, and cenfure *feelingly* expreffed ?

Mayhap the gentle reader will think no one could wifh to hurt, or dared calumniate, an author fo abounding in philanthropy and pity as myfelf. A man fo affectionately difpofed towards the happinefs of fociety, as to devote a portion of his time to the commendable employment of gently correcting the errors of fome, and boldly lafhing the vices of others, merely with the wifh to augment the felicity of the whole. Yet fuch beings exift, and in the very perfons of thofe who fhould, with all their power, protect the minds of the public from contamination, by difcountenancing all works that have fuch a tendency ; as well as fhield from infult, and, by their *fiat*, endeavour to propagate the circulation of thofe, that are calculated, *as in the prefent inflance*, to correct and mend the age.

But felf-intereft and private connection will, I forefee, rife paramount to candour and truth.

——————————ἐς ἀδὰν ἕλκομαι ἤδη. THEOCRIT.

Already I feel myfelf within their *predetermined* grafp. Nay, fpare me not moft upright judges ! Wait not for thofe *cogent* reafons that ever win your love, but which I fhall never deign to impart. Fall on at once ;—and let the world fee how an author fares when he fpeaks of you, or of your friends, according to your deferts ; and how lenient and how juft you are when neither praifed nor bribed.

CAUSES WHY NO FAVOUR IS EXPECTED FROM THE REVIEWERS.

THERMOMETER.

SCALE,—*from* 1 *to* 20.

		Self-interest.	Connection.	Natural furness; discovered when the writer is not known personally, and presumes to depend on the merit of his work *alone* for grateful sounds from a Reviewer's trumpet.
CRITICAL REVIEW. *Democratical.*	Mr. Godwin.........		17	16
	Mr. Holcroft.........	16	19	20
	Mr. Chalmers.......		12	20
BRITISH CRITIC. *Aristocratical.*	Mr. Nares...........		10	10
	Mr. Beloe............		14	12
	Dr. Parr.............	19		20
	Dr. Davis............		16	17
	Dr. Norbury........		12	17
MONTHLY REVIEW. *Amphibious.*	Dr. Thompson.....		18	10
	Mr. Pinkerton......		18	12
ANALYTICAL REVIEW *Levellers.*	Dr. Darwin.........		17	8
	Dr. Rees.............		18	12
	Mr. Belsham........		16	18
	Dr. Towers..........	12	14	14
	Dr. Aikin............		10	16
ENGLISH REVIEW.	Obsolete.			

Something like the above should always introduce a satirical production :[*] It not only preserves the judgment of men in general from being misled by the partial opinions of these *sons* of *Aristarchus*, but it precludes the necessity of having recourse to their writings, as such a thermometer shews exactly how the pulse of the Reviewer beats at the moment he is about to make his observations, and thence, naturally, what may be expected from such a disposition.

[*] It is recommended to the reader to peruse the whole of this poem with or without referring to the notes, as he deems it expedient, and finds it agreeable to himself. A certain *dabbler in Helicon*, whom, in a future publication, I shall, fearless of his threats, name *multa cum libertate*, has thought it proper to enjoin a primary simple reading of the po m.[†] His infantile injunction reminds me of a fair author, who lately printed some odes in the style of Pindar, as *she* was pleased to call them, by subscription; to which she prefixed a note, "Respectfully requesting the subscribers would permit her to wait on them, before they passed their judgment on the work, as the construction of the verse was such, that nobody could possibly decide on its merit, unless they had heard her read it."

[†] It also talks of originality. See Horace Aug. Ep. 1. lib. 2 for his *new* idea; see Sat. 1. lib. 2. for his *novel* mode of conveying satire, see Pope's Dunc. and his imit. of Hor. for both; and then see the *Pursuits of Literature*, for *original*—authors.

THE

PIN BASKET.

AGAIN, my Mufe, I wake the trembling lyre,

Again thy aid invoke, thy quick'ning fire!

Give me with force to ftrike my fav'rite ftring---

Grant that not wholly uninfpir'd I fing!

Forward the labours of thy Poet's brain ;

Once more be *Prompter* to his *Thefpian ftrain:*

So fhall thy altar of the plunder fhare,

And oft a *fatted calf* be offer'd there.*

Fear not my vow! I'll folve it o'er and o'er---

No Smithfield drover has a richer ftore.

Proceed! Come, join my ftandard, truft my word,

And let's together dafh amid the herd. .

---

* Left the Mufe, or any body elfe, fhould be furprifed at fuch a promife from a poet, you are entreated to confider, that he intends performing it out of *his ideal,* and not out of his *fubftantial* property. This explanation will alfo ferve to calm the apprehenfions of his fock and bufkin friends—airy nothings !

C .

No o'er-fed bard, no venal fongfter I;

Let Peter penfion'd* fing, and meet the eye,

As fat† as any pig, in any ftye;

To me fuch looks belie the vot'ry of the Mufe,

Who breathes Parnaffian air, and quaffs th' Olympian dews,

And would proclaim to all (a femblance fit)

More of the Cutting Butcher than the wit.

Farewel to fong, when poets touch the pelf,

Adieu to Peter then, now batt'ning on the fhelf.‡

* Whether Peter Pindar was ever penfioned, or whether he received that penfion for more than one or two years, or whether he receives it ftill, is no bufi-nefs of ours. But certain it is, we incline to think that Peter does enjoy *his fop;* not only from *his condition,* but from the wifdom with which adminiftration have always been obferved to deal out their rewards. Burke fhall be muzzled with a penfion when he has not a tooth left, and Peter bribed to hold his peace when he has not a word more to fay. It would appear from this, that minifters reward lefs for the good of their country (as they do it when all the mifchief's done) than from a conviction, in their own minds, that thofe whom they reward are as great rogues as themfelves, and as much entitled to partake of the prey.

† 'Tis as diftreffing to fee a poet *run to belly,* " *latamque trahens inglorius alvum,*" as to hear
" A little, round, fat, greafy man of God,"
like Dr. Towers, preaching temperance, prayer, and fafting, from the pulpit.

‡ Treafury fhelf.

Not fo with me, or I were perhaps as dull*---

Lord knows the time when I'd a belly full!

No! thin and fleek---in rare fine running order

My honeft Mufe has kept me---Heaven reward her!

The doctor's gouty leg (I ride a feather)

Would weigh my Pegafus and me together.

But now I pant impatient for the round,

And now I feem to touch the diftant ground;

---

* We do not think our author is here paying himfelf any great compliment. The following anecdote of Peter will fhew how much miftaken the world has been in his ability. At a time when he was not fo completely " Epicuri de grege porcus," the great Pindar, the mighty bard, condefcended, in great humility, to accept an engagement at two or three pounds a week, to write paragraphs for a certain newfpaper. For which purpofe, he would go to the office, where he has often fat for hours together, and at laft brought forth one or two fpare paragraphs, and often been unable to produce any. He was foon difmiffed, as an unprofitable fubject. From his late poetical attempts, we know nothing which he can be better compared to than to a ftreet organ, which, having got through its dozen tunes, can only repeat the fame ftrains. We cannot here refrain from fubjoining a note of his, which now, as it happens, applies to no one better than to himfelf. " Unfortunately for poor John," his name is John Wolcott, " every book that he has publifhed lately has been poffeffed of fo much of the *vis inertiæ*, as not to be able (if I may ufe the bookfellers' phrafe) to move off." We have feen, in particular, two or three of his recent publications ready to *be moved off*, at feveral ftalls (if any body would take the trouble to move them) much under (not their value) but the original price.

All obſtacles appear already croſt,
Yet ere I ſtart, *near thirty lines* are loſt.*

Suppoſe me then, good folks, with fancy heated,
Upon my tripod in the attic ſeated;
Pen, ink, and paper, all before me laid,
The ſimple tools of my immortal trade;
With chin upon my thumb and finger lolling,
And eye already fixt, prepar'd for rolling---
When at my door, a tap! alarmed I hear,
And all my well-plann'd thoughts diſſolve to air:
A bailiff ſure! I knew *his tap*, methought,
Then ſoftly creeping on, and breathing ſhort,
(As much in fear, juſt then, of ſuch detection
As I have ſeen St. Stephen's at election†)

---

* Theſe verſes are partly the tranſlation of Pope. Statius cannot be ſaid to
be ſo happy in his application as our poet.

" Stare loco neſcit, pereunt veſtigia mille
" Ante fugam, abſentemque ferit gravis ungula campum."

† The gentlemen of that *ſacred houſe* (as Mr. Burke calls it) are not a little
alarmed at this event; although they are well aſſured of being returned for one

[13]

I peep'd, but faw I had no caufe to tremble,

So ope'd my portal wide, and in ftalk'd KEMBLE.

Thinking I could not now be aught but civil,

(Though I would full as foon have feen the devil)

I begg'd he'd fit---as foon 'twas done as faid---

He on the ftool, and I upon the bed.*

Then thus began the man of tragic-gaze,

With Jefuitic† grin, and meafur'd phrafe.

houfe or the other: v. gr. If they are rejected by their conftituents, their creditors are always *ready to return them for the Bench.*

* Pafquin is not the firft great man who has (for the beft of all reafons) received company fitting on his bed. Theodore, King of Corfica, when in the Bench for debt, actually held his levees there regularly, and received his courtiers fitting on a femi-tent bed, the head of which forming a canopy, added to the dignity of his fituation. We think that poor Theodore was a type of what we might expect to fee in the prefent MARLBOROUGH family, were they reduced to a ftate of equal indigence. They would ftill retain all their vain oftentation, and affected confequence. O the empty pride and vanity of man!

    " De tous les animaux qui s' élevent dans l' air,
    " Qui marchent fur la terre; ou nagent dans la mer,
    " De Paris au Perou, du Japon jufqu á Rome,
    " Le plus fot animal, a mon avis, c'eft l' homme.

† Mr. Kemble was brought up at St. Omer's, a town in French Flanders, and

D

KEMBLE.

" So, fo, the GREEN-ROOM's in a pretty rout,

" And long to know what 'tis that you're about.

" Tell me, my PASQUIN, as a friend I afk it,

" Who is't you mean to cram into your BASKET?

intended to have been made a prieft in that famous religious order in the Romifh church called Jefuits. For reafons, unknown to us, this idea was fuperfeded ; though, from the conduct, temper of mind, and confonant affections, he has, and ftill continues to exhibit, we have no doubt that he is well verfed in the *Secreta Monita Societatis Jefu*, has taken *them to heart*, and would have done *great honour* to the fect. Among other precepts which this virtuous order inculcates, we find the following.

" The fociety may traffic, and borrow, and lend money, but never *without a profpect of certain and abundant* gain.

" In whatever places the members refide, they muft provide a phyfican, who is firm to the intereft of the fociety, by whom they *may be recommended* and called in to the fick, *efpecially fuch as are paft hopes of recovery.*

" Women who complain of their hufbands, muft be inftructed fecretly to withdraw a fum of money, that by *making an offering thereof to God*, they may *expiate the crimes of their finful helpmates.*

" They are *to worm themfelves*, by the intereft of others, into honourable embaffies, which may give them an opportunity of *recommending themfelves* and *their fociety.*

" Not me, I hope. Confider! Heaven preferve you!

" Would to my heart my friend, that I could ferve you."*

PASQUIN.

" Away with all fuch hypocritic ftuff!

" I will not take a felfifh bribe, to puff

" The undeferving through the lift'ning town,

" Above the man whom worth and merit own.

" Go, go, to BOADEN, or to TAYLOR† hie,

" Thofe *bards of all work* will, as wont, comply ;

---

* This is perfectly in character : full of fervility where he fears ; arrogant and overbearing where he's in power.

† John Taylor, or Jack Taylor, a relation of J. P. Kemble, formerly did the dirty work, in the puffing way, in the True Briton, for the wholebody of his kindred. Befides this, he is a dentift ; and then he writes, or rather cobbles, prologues for any body that will accept of them. It has been faid, that he even offered money to an oppofite neighbour, to let him write one to a piece of his. In fine, he is a complete *bard of all work*, not very diffimilar to Hoare's Dicky Goffip ;--- for, in the firft place, as a newfpaper-man, he fits in the office and *cuts out* matter from other papers to fill up his mafters ; then, as a dentift, he *draws out* ; next, as an eternal gabbler, he generally *routs out* all the companies he gets into ; and laftly, as a filly trifling fellow, he will be *laid out* to the great comfort of fociety.

" Or to the *Times*, where thy right worthy friend,

" Does with his darling unlick'd cub contend,

" And faith 'twould puzzle Wifdom's felf to tell

" The greateft fool, they act their parts fo well.*

" Off to thofe honeft prints, that virtuous hoft,

" Who ever praife him beft, who pays them moft.†

---

* It is certain there never was fuch a jolter-headed family as this. The old man has doubtlefs fcraped together fome pelf, and fo might any man that would ftoop to the fame means. Let a recent anecdote of him fhew how excellently he combines the fool and ————— thus it is.

A libel having appeared in his paper againft a foreigner, he was profecuted, and perceiving he muft be caft, made overtures to the gentleman, who, with proper indignation, refufed them, declaring, he would have ftrict juftice, and nothing lefs, for the defamation he had experienced. Old W. with that tender folicitude which every parent fhould feel for the property he intends for his children, went immediately to Mr. Dundas, who, at the requeft of the proprietor of a paper in the pay of Mr. Pitt, inftantly ordered the injured foreigner, at the moment of retribution, to quit the kingdom.

Young Hopeful pretends to be a writer, and keeps up his credit, with their *printer* and THE DEVILS (his, and his papa's beft friends) by getting fome of his acquaintance, who amufe themfelves with writing fcraps of poetry, &c. to fend them to him, which he then copies, and gives up for his own. That fuch a father fhould doat on fuch a fon can be no wonder.

" Afinus afino, et fus fui pulcher."

† Newfpaper men will generally be found as void of principle and difreputable, proud and ignorant, as any people on the face of the earth. Reporters of fpeeches

" Still let us hear you tones fepulchral bray,

" And then be told ' How wonderful you play;'*

" Deceive the world, out-lie all contradiction,

" And fwear yourfelf a play'r 'gainft conviction."

KEMBLE.

" Be calm, my friend!"

PASQUIN.

" Be juft, 'tis true, you know it!"

KEMBLE.

" That you're the beft of men, and fweeteft poet.

made in the Houfe of Commons, in particular, are a mechanical, felf-opiniated, baftard brood of dunghills, who can only crow when thofe luminaries rife; never at the call of genius; but at the gnawings of an empty belly: who have not a thought of their own which is not as low, groveling and obnoxious as the *contemptible thing* they are *for ever thinking about.*

* This is continually the cafe. You fhall go to the play and fee (if you can keep your eyes open) not only Kemble, but others, who can pay for it, fleep through their parts; and the next morning, the firft thing you read fhall be " How amazingly great fuch an one was in fuch a part, &c." To prove more clearly how premeditated a bufinefs it is, we have feveral times read a pompous account of fome actor's or actrefs's performance, for whom we have heard an apology made the evening before, as being incapable of playing from indifpofition. The fact is, the fellow, whoever he is, inftead of going to the *play-houfe*, writes the ftipulated

E

" I've brib'd, I own, but merely 'twas, forfooth,

" To keep thofe *lying prints* from telling *truth.*

lines previous to the commencement of the play, and then betakes himfelf to the
ale-houfe, to fpend the profits along with his comrades ;

A crew that Falftaff's felf would blufh to own.

The critics of the modern ftage are thus diftinguifhed.

Parfon Rofe, in the Times, for puerile puns, no wit, and as much judgment.

Parfon Efte, in the Telegraph, for a clofe imitation of the ftyle of Van Butchell.

Parfon Armftrong, in the Chronicle, for dull prolixity, or Caledonian humour.
(He calls his efforts *criticifms*, but the parfon lies—under an error; they
are literally illiterate *fermons.*) Lord Mountmorres alfo fometimes illu-
mines the Chronicle with a critique.

Jack Taylor, in the True Briton, (and every where elfe) for inanity.

Thady Byrne, in the Herald, for *Irifh* originality. We have feen, on feveral
occalions, fome very pointed and judicious remarks in this paper from
the pen of M'Donnel—we wifh we were indulged with them more re-
peatedly.

Boaden, in the oracle, for *great big words*, which he often mifappropriates, and an
unintelligible affectation of profundity.

Dalmerda, in the Gazetteer, for very neat language, and obfervations fraught with
much critical difcernment.

Pollio, or *Litchfield*, in the Morning Poft, for the old ideas of his contemporaries
newly varnifhed, tedious dilatation, and blunt abufe of thofe who will
not condefcend *to court his* favour.

Bourne, in the Obferver, for ftrictures only worthy of the writer.

" What could I do? altho' fo much you flout it,

" There's not a manager could live without it.

" What think you otherwife could e'er induce

" That lump of ignorance, HARRIS, to produce

" BATE DUDLEY's* ribaldry, or HURLSTONE's† trafh,

" But that it ferv'd for bribe, and fav'd his cafh.

Barr, in Ayres' Sunday, for fome marks of judgment and wit devoid of polifh.

Arnold, Jun. late Editor of the Tomahawk, in Bell's Weekly, for a favage deter-mination to write in fpite of common fenfe, and want of readers.

* *Bate Dudley* being the editor of the Morning Herald, was enabled, through an indifcriminate commendation of whatever appeared at Covent Garden, to prevail on the manager to bring forward two or three of his compofitions, which were perhaps the moft infipid, uninterefting nonfenfe that ever difgraced a ftage.

He has the prefumption to fancy he can imitate the writings of Shakfpeare. Even in like manner had that *mighty critic*, Mr. Boaden ; who could accept Ireland's *abfurd jargon*, for the *winged words* (as Homer has it) of our *deathlefs bard.* Each thinks himfelf a phœnix—fo they are—fuch as we fee over the door of the Herald office—*phœnixes without heads*.

† *Mr. Hurlftone*, the book-keeper at the office of this paper, is a good natured fellow, but who, beyond his occupation, does not know his right hand from his left. Yet, " like mafter, like man," he alfo muft be writing plays, and in truth were it any praife to him) *has written them as well.*

" Or BOADEN's tragic Mufe create a laugh,

" Unlefs he paid his way in paragraph.*

" Or WALTERS fill whole boxes at the play---

" Lord help your foul, you do not think they pay!

" But now my managerial part is done,

" And ftrange! I don't regret my fceptre gone!

" They had *my fervices,* and *fifter's too,*

" While yet the treafury could boaft *a fous;*

---

* Had *Mr. Boaden* continued, what he originally was, a banker's clerk, we fhould like to know what kind of *acceptation* his *foporific pills* would have received from Harris? But allowing him his due, we muft fay that, although as dull a matter-of-fact genius as ever ftood behind a counter, he has managed, by fome means, to infufe into his *tragedies* a certain *portion of humour,* paft all poffibility of feeing without a fmile. We defy any man to fit out the " *Secret Tribunal*" without laughing; efpecially at the *grand cataftrophe,* where the inquifitors affembled, form as fine a picture of a watch-houfe at five in the morning, as ever was feen. Mr. B. however, had little to plume himfelf on his intereft with the manager in this inftance, fince he had feventy pounds to pay for empty benches, or *rather for his empty noddle.*

When Mr. Harris announced this deficiency to him, he is faid to have affumed the very air of the *oraculous prieftefs,* at the Oracle office, which fo alarmed Harris that he inftantly forgave him the debt his *melancholy Mufe* had contracted. The *provifo* that attended this remiffion we have not heard. Mr. B. we *are forry to un-*

" And *tragedy*, whate'er the public fancies,

" Much *best became* the *company's finances*.*

" Can HARRIS† then, or COLMAN e'er afpire,

" To half my talents, genius, wit, and fire?

---

derftand, has taken to write comedy, and has actually written one called *The Baotian Wit.* . If he continues in this mind;

> " Farewel mirth and jollity, ,
> " Smiles no more we've need of thee."

* Some people fay that Mr. Kemble abounds in wit, when he pleafes to indulge himfelf. This feems to be a lucky moment. Still we may fay of him with Hudibras, when we recollect his various *fuccefsful* alterations of plays, and that original *fpark*, that *blaze* of genius, the *luminous* Lodoifka. .

> " We grant he has wit,
> " But's very fhie of ufing it,
> " As being loath to wear it out ;
> " And therefore bears it not about,
> " Unlefs on holidays, or fo, .
> "'As men their beft apparel do."

† If Harris has not fo much genius as Kemble; which is very doubtful, he certainly may conteft the palm with him for mean artifice and deceit. Deceit feems in a manner fated to people in their fituation. We fhall give an example of it in Harris. Juft at the time Mr. Hoare, at his particular requeft, gave him the Lock and Key, and it was brought out, Mrs. Serres, who had a part in it, had written to Harris at Uxbridge about an engagement ; he anfwering her letter, and one from Lewis by the fame poft, in hafte, directed them reverfely. Mrs. Serres received, as fhe expected, a letter addreffed to her, which ran to the following effect.

F

" Have not I acted, writ, and alter'd* plays,

" Been clapp'd! been damn'd!---*now shan't I have your praise?*"

PASQUIN.

" Thus thou, by here recounting others ailings,

" Would'ft toil to weave a cloak to hide thy failings.

" Dear Lewis,

" I am very much amazed to hear from you that Hoare's farce met with a cool reception--I thought it was a better piece. Damn that Mrs. Serres, I wifh fhe had never come into the houfe; fhe's an eternal plague to me. We muft get rid of her fomehow or another.

" Yours, &c.
" T. Harris."

The feelings of Mrs. S. may eafily be conceived; but fhe had fcarcely recovered herfelf when Lewis came on the ftage, where fhe was, grinning and whimpering in his ufual way, " Here is your letter, madam! Spofe you've one intended for me. Droll miftake egad!" She then read,

" Dear Madam,

" I am a little bufy at prefent, but fhall be in town in a day or two, when you fhall have every thing fettled to your wifh.

" Yours, &c.
" T. Harris."

* Mr. K. lately altered one of Mr. Wycherly's plays, in which he *modeftly* filled the *plain dealer* himfelf, for the firft time of his acting that part in our remem-brance. He was feen but twice in this character.

" Be HARRIS ignorant, as you declare,

" And obſtinate as any Ruſſian bear;*

" What tho' a monkey, as the ſtory goes,

" Alone has power to lead him by the noſe:†

" No mighty diſagreement I divine,

" Except he always keeps the ſtupid line,

" And thou art ſomewhat more a fool in wine.‡

" Yet mention not, with impious tongue, thy name

" With his, which Time ſhall glory to proclaim,

" And *honeſt critics* conſecrate to fame!

* Obſtinacy and ignorance are inſeparable, and few people ever carried theſe amiable qualities to a higher degree of perfection than the manager of Covent Garden theatre.

† One fool is known to have greater power over another than all the logic in the world. Lewis is ſaid to be able to do with him whatever he liſts, and really he deſerves no little credit for it, if, as ſome one obſerves, " To keep a fool conſtantly in good humour with himſelf, and with others, is no eaſy taſk."

‡ This is a very excellent diſtinction. Mr. K. when he is ſober, will ſit for hours without ſaying a word : but no ſooner has he drank a quantity, and he will drink immoderately, than he'll ſtart from his ſeat, and ſwear he'll be a member of Parliament; then fancy himſelf in *the houſe*, and begin to declaim, run on a parcel of unintelligible nonſenſe, and at length ſit down as contented with himſelf, and perhaps with as much title, as General Tarleton, or Chicken Taylor.— " Quid non ebrietas deſignat," ſays Horace.

" BOADEN* may fneer, and tedious POLLIO† fcribble,

" With foul detraction thro' dull columns dribble;

* Mr. Boaden's pitiful enmity to Mr. Colman, does not arife only from the envious eyes with which he views Mr. C's fuperior abilities, but alfo from his having given a proof of his difcernment and careful attention to the amufement of the public, in refufing a farce prefented to him, called Ofmyn and Daraxa ; performed afterwards at the great theatre in the Haymarket, previous to the building of new Drury, and defervedly damned. *Hinc illæ lachrymæ.* Ever fince he has exercifed his impotent malignity againft a man who is far above the reach of his flander.

Every thing concerning the *Little Theatre*, which appears in the Oracle, is written under the head *Little Houfe.* We fhould be at a lofs to conceive what this meant, were we not certain that Mr. B. writes the criticifms himfelf, and that this is a very proper direction where to take them to.·

† Pollio, or a Mr. Litchfield, is a young man belonging to fome office about town, whofe employers not giving, or having fufficient bufinefs to take up the whole of his time, feeks a further occupation in fcribbling for newfpapers, at fome inconfiderable ftipend. He formerly wrote, what he calls, critiques for the Publican's Advertifer, but being difmiffed from that paper, he now does them for the Morning Poft. He alfo contributes occafionally to a trifling publication, called the Monthly Mirror. In thefe feveral things he has uniformly abufed Mr. Colman and his productions. As this cannot have arifen from any refufal of a piece or any thing of that kind on the part of Mr. C.—he being incapable of writing any thing except dull effays for magazines, and long-winded remarks for newfpapers, which nobody reads—we cannot attribute it to aught but that he would ferve the wound rankling in the bofom of Mr. Boaden, with whom, from the manner they appear to play into each other's hands, we have no doubt he is clofely connected. Notwithftanding,

" They fight a war of waves againft a rock,"

" But impotent they ſtrive, with pigmy blow,

" To beat the firm-fix'd bay from COLMAN'S brow;

" It lives, ſhall flouriſh, ſpite of Envy's blaſt.

" For gain'd by merit it with time ſhall laſt!

" Thou, pining at his worth, his wily friend,*

" Did'ſt dare to injure what thou could'ſt not mend.†

we cannot ſuppoſe that either will deſiſt, while the one has a grudge to gratify, and empty columns to fill, and the other no alternative to paſs his time.

In the ſummer this young ſpark is infected with the *ſpouting inſania,* and goes to different parts of the country, where he ſtruts his hour to the great amuſement of—himſelf.

* Mr. K. has, in more inſtances than one, under the maſk of friendſhip, be-trayed and ill-treated Mr. Colman. When Mr. C. was writing his excellent play of the Mountaineers, K. chanced to be on a viſit at his houſe, and having read part of the character of Octavian, was ſo delighted with it, that he entreated to play it at the little theatre. Mr. C. aſſured him that he could not afford him ſuch a ſalary as he would demand: to which he replied, " that he would play it for nothing, *for he knew it would be the making of him.*"—" Well," was the rejoinder, " if it will ſerve you, I will work up the character purpoſely for you, and give you twelve pounds a week." Kemble after this abuſed Mr. Colman, and ſaid, he had paid him like a beggar.—Ingratum odi!

† By acting worſe than he generally does, Mr. K. has often, but not always without reprobation, attempted to ſet the performance of an author he diſliked in the worſt light. Witneſs his execrable conduct during the repreſentation of Ire-

G

land's Vortigern! Though we are very willing to condemn this as a deferving production, we cannot but defpife fuch Jefuitical cunning in an actor. 'Twas the
fame when he played in the Iron Cheft. Had he laboured under fuch a fevere
indifpofition as he affected, why did he not keep his chamber? Why did he make
his appearance only to injure a meritorious work? Take this reply,—If he was as
ill as he feemed, he merely took that opportunity of doing more covertly, what, had
he been well, as in Vortigern, he intended to attempt. But notwithftanding all
the foul means that may have been, or can be ufed, to take away from the value of
the Iron Cheft, which I do contend contains much beautiful and mafterly writing,
or to blur the well-earned reputation of Mr. Colman as a writer, the time fhall
come when his *contemporary dramatic authors*, to ufe Falftaff's phrafe, " Shall all
fhew like *gilt two-pences* to him; and he in the clear fky of fame."

Mr. C. in his preface to his Iron Cheft, has ably explained to the world the
caufe of its mal-fuccefs, at Drury Lane Theatre; and Mr. Ellifton, by an *honeft*
exertion of powers, which promife foon to eclipfe the *partial* merit of his fraternity,
has confirmed the truth of every affertion, drawing down from frequent unbiaffed
audiences, at the Haymarket, the meed which envy and knavery had till then the
fortune to withhold from the out-ftretched hand of juftice.

With all thefe convincing arguments in favour of its merit, Mr. C. muft
laugh at the pointlefs rage of *Garretteers*, who, under the mafk of impartial criti-
cifm, gratify, if not fome latent enmity, fome lurking malice; at leaft *attempt* to
gratify the cravings of an hungry belly.

Still they yelp! ftill they fpit their fpite! ftill their envious bills are pecking
at his fame! and what does it all prove? Juft as much with him as with refpect
to fruit, " That is ufually found to be the fweeteft, which the birds have pecked at
the moft."

We do not find ourfelves difpofed to conclude this note, without touching
lightly upon fome very illiberal comments made by a writer in the Monthly Mir-

ror, (a Mr. Litchfield we fufpect) on the laft production of Mr. Colman. He fingles out thefe verfes, which he ftrives to ridicule and pervert.

> " Heaven and earth!
> " Let my pure flame of honour fhine in ftory
> " When I am cold in death; and the flow fire
> " That wears my vitals *now*, will no more move me,
> " Than 'twould a corpfe within a monument."

Which verfes, divefted of their poetical habiliment, have this very fenfible and intelligible fignification.

" Oh heaven! Let me but think, that, when I am no more, my fame fhall live unfullied; and the anguifh of mind, which *now*, *at this moment*, preys upon my vitals, occafioned by the fear I entertain of the reverfe, will no more afflict me, than it would a body incapable of fufferance."

The little adverb NOW, it feems, *ex induftriâ*, efcaped this fapient commentator, who, by the further aid of *italics* and *falfe punctuation*, would fain make us believe that Mr. C. intended Sir Edward Mortimer fhould fay,

" That when he was dead, he fhould be no more fufceptible of pain or remorfe, than any other corpfe."

Genius of fophiftication! was there ever fuch mifreprefentation as this?

We have neither room nor inclination to follow this angry critic, *Blundering for his purpofe*, through the abfurdity and fallacioufnefs of all his malicious mifacceptations of Mr. C's fenfe, but we cannot help noticing a literary impofition, in the conftant ufe of the prefent writer, by which, with fome people, he may be miftaken for a man of deep reading.

Inftances of it in him are numberlefs; but the few which offer themfelves on the very page now before us will ferve, as well as many more, to explain our meaning.

In *torturing* the paſſage juſt treated of, he makes this obſervation.

" FLAME," ſays Sir Iſaac Newton, " IF WE RECOLLECT RIGHT, is but a va-pour, an exhalation heated red hot," and thus Milton :

" Vapour, and miſt, and exhalation hot."

" *If we recollect right !*" Now from this, who would not ſuppoſe that he was perfectly verſed in Sir Iſaac, and had Milton by heart ? when at the ſame time it is odds he has not read the laſt, and a thouſand to one he never *ſaw* the former. 'Tis yet ſtrange ; but to him who poſſeſſes a Johnſon's dictionary, the juggle ſtands confeſt. *Flame* is the ſubject ! turn to *flame* in the Doctor's folio edition.

FLAME, n. s. Is not a *flame* a vapour, fume, or exhalation heated red hot ? Newton."

As Mr. C. talks of " a flame ſhining in ſtory," it was as well not to give any more of the quotation, which proceeds thus, " red hot, that is, ſo hot as to ſhine."

The epithet *pure*, applied to *flame*, he, certainly from never having read the poets, deems improper. And as Doctor Johnſon gives it againſt him under ſeveral words, we are thence led to ſuppoſe that he had recourſe for his information, in this inſtance, to Mother Johnſon's dictionary, where he could hardly expect to find *pure flame*.

Well, ſomething is ſtill wanting on *the ſubject*. Flame is but a *vapour*, ac-cording to Newton. See VAPOUR. Here we have what we need.

" Vapour, and miſt, and exhalation hot."   *Milton, John. Dict.*

" Naturaliſts," ſays he, in a period juſt before this, " have *informed* us that ſprings break out from the top of hills, &c. &c." Had he acknowledged that Dr. Johnſon *informed* him ſo under the word *ſprings*, we would believe him.

" Again, in the ſame page, we find a pretty anecdote of Biſhop Wilkins, who did not queſtion but the time would come, when it would be as uſual to hear a

" Away, incapable of generous deed!

" Yet mark you firſt, the lines I'd have you heed.

" '*Rejeɛt the praiſes you can ne'er preſerve,

" ' Believe not what you pay for you deſerve.

" ' Survey thy ſoul, not what thou doſt appear,

" ' But what thou art---and find the beggar there."

This ſaid, with haſte, his hat he riſing took,
And left the room with curs'd Meduſan look.

man call for his *wings*, when he is going a journey, as then it was to call for his *boots*. See this under the word *Boot*.

A little beyond another quotation is required to *help out*. Pope's a very good Poet, and a line from him will embelliſh.

> " None but himſelf can be his parallel."

See Parallel.

All theſe occur in the ſhort ſpace of two pages! and we think it would be unneceſſary to purſue him any further, as they will ſufficiently ſhew, that *making* eſſays, &c. to men who have recourſe to ſuch auxiliaries, is a taſk of but very little difficulty, and worthy of but very moderate praiſe.

> * " Reſpue quod non es: tollat ſua munera cerdo:
> " Tecum habita, et nòris quam ſit tibi curta ſupellex."
> PERSIUS.

H .

" Farewel to KEMBLE! how the truth will fting!"

Exclaim'd the bard, and fmooth'd his ruffled wing.

For honeft fervor had diftrub'd him more, ⎫

Than milk-maids are, when you rub out the fcore, ⎬

Or LADY LADE, when told---her knight is poor.* ⎭

Or LEEDS and MULGRAVE, when you laugh to fee

Them work away as COBB and company.†

---

* Lady Lade, though Sir John keeps a continual auction in his houfe, cannot bear to hear that he is growing poor. Thofe who fee the knight and his lady fitting at the opera, as far apart as their box will permit, and *fafhionable decency* orders married folks to obferve, will fcarcely credit, what is an abfolute fact, that Sir John hardly ever lets a day efcape without writing billet-doux to his fair fpoufe, and will pine and take on like any Arcadian fwain, if fhe will not fmile upon him; which favour he ftill buys, when he has any money. Her ladyfhip, who certainly muft know beft, calls him an old fool, and tells every body that he writes love letters to her.

Black Davis, we are forry to fay, is proving poor Sir John, with all his expe- rience, to be ftill a pigeon.

† Lord Mulgrave, Mr. Cobb, and the Duke of Leeds, together, produced that wonderful effort of genius, *The Firft of June.* Cobb wrote the dialogue, Leeds and Mulgrave the fongs. What may we not expect from fuch a triumvi- rate with perfeverance !

Or HANGER* if you joke him on his book,

Or even fay he has a hanging look.

Or DOCTOR PARR,† when afk'd a civil queftion,

Who'll growl and grunt, and eat paft all digeftion.

* Lieutenant Colonel George Hanger, has lately written a Pamphlet entitled MILITARY REFLECTIONS, compofed as he walked up and down Bond-Street and Pall-Mall. We wifh the Colonel much fuccefs in his *literary perambulations,* and have no hefitation in thinking, that he will not ceafe from his labours until he has written as many books as—he has read.

† There is not a more proud, overbearing, unfociable being in exiftence than Parr. Puffed up with pedantry, and falfe notions of his confequence, he is wanting in common civility to almoft every body. We remember dining at a friend's houfe fome time fince, where the Doctor was prefent, and who, be-ing the greateft ftranger, was of courfe treated with the moft attention. There happened to be fifh at the head of the table, and beef at the bottom. The lady of the houfe fent him fome fifh ; upon which he peevifhly exclaimed, " I am not a pifcivorous animal—I never eat fifh." She then begged her neighbour to help him to fome beef ; but before that could be done, he growled out, " I hate beef." " Good God!" faid the lady to a friend who had brought the Doctor unexpectedly, " this is very unfortunate, for you really fee your dinner—what can I do ?"—" Never mind, leave him alone," faid the gentleman, " he'll come round beft by himfelf!" and fure enough he did, for when he perceived how they were difpofed to treat him, he began upon the beef, and eat, at leaft, as much as two of us.

Before this memorable dinner, the gentleman in whofe houfe he was, coming up to Dr. Parr, who was ftanding at the window, looking over the True Briton, " What do you think of that paper, Sir ?" faid he. " Why I think Sir," replied he, sternly, "that none but fools take it in, and none but fools read it." The gentleman, quite thunderstruck at *such politeness*, had not the presence of mind to add, " that he believed so, from seeing it in the Doctor's hands."

Parr, as it was said of Dr. Johnson, whom he affects to imitate, and of whose failings he certainly affords no bad idea, is like a ghost—he never speaks till he is spoken to. But here the simile of the ghost *vanishes*.

When Johnson was roused, though a bear in manners and in seeming,

" Ye Gods how he would talk !"

How would he blend instruction with delight ! The fascination of his elo-quence charmed, though it reproved, and " truth came mended from his tongue."

" Not by Hæmonian hills the Thracian bard,
" Nor awful Phœbus was on Pindus heard,
" With deeper silence and with more regard."

His auditors would lift,

" Till unperceiv'd the heavens with stars were hung,
" And sudden night surpris'd the yet unfinish'd song."

Parr, when stirred, merely grunts out a contemptuous reply, rubs his paws, and goes to sleep again.

Οὐδέ μιν φόρμυγγες ὕπω
μέφιζι κοινωνίαν
Μαλθακὰν παίδων ἑάροισι ἔιχονται.
PINDAR Pyth. 1. Epod. v.

" Him therefore nor in *sweet society*,
" —————— conversing ever name :
" Nor with the harp's delightful melody
" Mingle his odious *inharmonious fame*."   WEST.

More was not Cowflip mov'd, when fet a raving

By DERBY,* who declar'd fhe wanted fhaving,

And fwore as fhe came off the ftage—all puffing,

That fhe'd play Falftaff better—without ftuffing.†

Or fimple ARNOLD, when, in harmlefs fun,

You fmile to hear him praife his filly fon‡.

---

* This fprightly little lord is always cracking his good things on her ladyfhip. They often *play together* at the Margravine of Anfpach's puppet fhew. He enacts Punch, fhe his Wife, and the Margrave on particular occafions *plays the Devil.* This joke of his could not have been at all agreeable to Cowflip, for this reafon— That *true jefts* are of all others the leaft entertaining—*to thofe whom they concern.*

† Cowflip, is a nick-name given to Lady Buckinghamfhire, ever fince fhe attempted that character at the Margravine's. His lordfhip meant fhe would play Falftaff better, being able to fay, at any time, with propriety,

" No quips now, Piftol ; indeed I am in the wafte two yards about ;
" but I am now about no wafte : I am about thrift."

And fhe is really thriving every day. But can it be a matter of furprife, when we inform you, her ladyfhip declared to us one night at the opera, " That fhe had her own cows driven to the door every morning ; and, that otherwife, although doatingly fond of tea, fhe could never drink a drop." Thus performing by the aid of milk, what Sir John effected with fack.

‡ Doctor Arnold is an honeft man, and now and then a good compofer; next, in our opinion, with fome interval between, to Shields. The Doctor's fimplicity of foul, and blind affection for his fon, are, though natural, often highly ridiculous.

I

Now fing we on, in fmooth harmonious ftrain,

The world in arms!—the mimic world I mean,

And give the final touch, to this our Thefpian fcene.

New Drury firft appears, in clamourous hum,

Like Stock Exchange, when fettling day is come!

All ready there, with claims in dread array—

All—all— but thofe who fhould be there to pay.

What wonder then if *waddling* fome fhould quit,

Full well affur'd—*ex nihilo nil fit.**

Benfley retires! and him the Mufe affords

A juft eulogium, and his worth records.

O! how fhe joys to praife!---compell'd fhe rails,

But yields with zeal when merit fills her fails.

Holcroft, talking with the old man one evening, in our company, about the Little Theatre, afked him---" Whether they had any thing coming out there?" " No," faid he, " I don't hear of any thing, except a play of Cumberland's. Sentiment, dull fentiment---*hot toaft in July*---Can't run long."---" They are badly off indeed then," was the reply. " Why no---my fon, my boy is at work for 'em. Day and night, night and day, he's at it---he'll keep them a going.

* Others, who have nowhere elfe to go, remain and confole themfelves, we imagine, by replying to thofe who make this obfervation---*Ex Nilo Mofes fit.*

*BENSLEY and POPE adieu! the ſtage ſhall find
You've ſcarce left aught of greater price behind.
But KING, ſhall KING,† the veteran, begone,
While yet *his legs* will *bear him off and on?*
Forbid it Juſtice---and his cauſe eſpouſe---
Some Goth or Vandal's ſure got in the houſe!
" True! true! 'tis thus the worn-out actor fares,"
Liſp'd honeſt WALDRON, coming up the ſtairs.

WALDRON.

" Good Maſter PASQUIN—O they've uſed me foul!
" I'm off!"‡

PASQUIN.

" I would you were with all my foul!

* Mr. Benſley and Miſs Pope make their final exit with nearly as much reputation as players, and with full as much private eſteem, for honor and integrity, as any they leave will find it poſſible to effect.

† We hear with much concern that King is diſmiſſed from Drury Lane. We hope it is not true. If he be obliged to reſign, through want of *bodily* powers, we cannot lament his loſs too much. If we are robbed of him by the blindneſs, or what not, of managers, we cannot condemn them ſufficiently for ingratitude to him, and for depriving us of ſo valuable an ornament to the Britiſh ſtage.

‡ Waldron is alſo caſhiered. He is an uſeful, though by no means a brilliant

" Well, as you're here, come fit ye, fit ye down,

" And let us hear what's ftirring 'bout the town."

WALDRON.

" What, war or peace? For peace the people figh,

" But all in vain, there's no one heeds their cry :

" Quicquid delirant reges, plecluntur Achivi." ⎫⎬⎭

PASQUIN.

" Pfhaw! Stuff! have done! you know what I've in hand,

" Thro' Drury failing—pray how lies the land?"

WALDRON.

" But badly faith, they've chang'd their mafter, true—

" *The Log's* difmifs'd, and they've *a Stork* in lieu ;*

player, and will doubtlefs be employed again. At his time of life he fhould not be thus banded about.

* The allufion to the fable is aptly enough introduced here. Kemble and his family might certainly be compared to a log, which, while he was manager, managed to keep every thing at a fland ftill. Thofe who are now at the helm, feem of an active *levelling* difpofition, and will, we think, either by a fortunate concurrence of events *mount*, or perhaps, by a more probable fuppofition, kick every *thing to the Devil.*

In a pamphlet, entitled " The Wreck of Weftminfter Abbey," we find the following epitaph on the *ci-devant* manager of Drury Lane theatre, which we think could not have been fo appofite a. any former period as at the prefent..

" Here rests
A vain, an infolent, but not a diverting,
rather a mourning vagabond,
A would-be Garrick, but ever was a K------- :
As a dramatift, he gained riches through the intereft of his
Siddonian Relative ;
but never acquired celebrity.
In his manner, ftiff, awkward, and conceited ;
In his utterance, turgid, precife, and univerfally monotonical ;
Affecting that which he ever did *but* affect,
The character of a Critic ;
Difregarding that which he ever fhould have regarded,
An appeal to the paffions, and an imitation
of the manners of Mankind.
When his fifter quitted the theatric boards, which fhe had trod
with uncommon and deferving reputation,
He was difcharged ;
The managers no longer being induced to preferve
a ftiff and infenfible mummy.
He died of the Cacoëthes Famæ, October 18—"
Ut nonnulli volunt ;
But as more have been heard to propound,
Of a complicate difeafe,
Called envy, rage, and difappointment :
Which firft feized him,
At the re-appearance, brilliant reception,
And merited fuccefs
Of the Iron Chest ;
To which he fell a melancholy object
Of pity and contempt.
K

" One *Lawyer Grubb**---in vain, poor fouls, we bawl out,

" He's in, and ere he's done, will *grub us* all out.

" There GIBBS fhall ftrain her little throat no more,

" And SEDGWICK,* *wood-work* SEDGWICK, ceafe to roar;

---

* Grubb is a cropt, ftupid, good-natured fellow, who had the happy fortune
to have a father, who was for many years clerk to the fifhmonger's company, and,
though no conjurer, was alfo a dealer in the black art, that is to fay, was an attor-
ney; in which profeffion he acquired a confiderable property, which his fon,
without being a conjurer, either will himfelf, or by the help of thofe he is now
connected with, foon find a mode of fpending. Young Grubb, for fo he likes to
be called, came forward very opportunely with fix thoufand pounds, when Sheridan
wanted " to make up a little fum to fend his poor relations in the country." For
which Mr. S. very handfomely gave him his own—verbal fecurity.

† The elegant, *unaffected, artlefs* deportment of Mr. Sedgwick on the ftage;
fo amiable in love fcenes, &c. &c. and unequalled by any but Mr. Boaden, at
the other houfe, muft certainly increafe the dolor of the public at the lofs of his
mufical powers.

One would not have thought that a manager could have difcharged fuch a *conftel-
lation* of excellence, fuch a *lump of harmony*, as Dignum is called, for the *trifling fault*,
which cuftom and Mr. John Palmer have almoft paffed into a law, of fcarcely ever
reading his part, till within half an hour of the time of performance, preferring
the more *refined delight* of driving a girl about in a gig.

" Thence BLAND,* by artful villany beguil'd,

" Bears the fweet notes that cheer'd the dreary *wild*.†

" Now follow CAULFIELD,‡ for thyfelf art free,

" We'll mark how far thy love will carry thee:

" Hence! on whom each honeft brow is fcowling,

" Nor loiter here, ' to bay the moon with howling.'

---

* Poor Bland! She is indeed deferving of our pity. Ruined by the vile artifice, the bafe feduction of Caulfield, we fhall foon lofe one of the fweeteft fingers,
and, as a finger, one of the beft comic actreffes, that ever walked the boards. She
is now about to crofs the Atlantic ; Mr. Caulfield's boafted love will confequently
be feen in its true colours.

† Wild, or wildernefs, was a title given to New Drury by the *fage* Mr.
Boaden. About which time Sheridan, who had heard this, was requefted to accept
a tragedy of Mr. Boaden's. " No, no," faid S. " He calls our Houfe a wildernefs ;—I don't mind letting the Oracle have his opinion, but I have a great objection to *permitting him to prove his words.*

‡ The ftage will not at all be injured by the abfence of this imprudent young
man. If he poffeffed any merit, it was as an imitator ; a fpecies of exhibition
managers do not confult their own intereft by encouraging. Many excellent per-
formers, who have, as is common to all people, either fome peculiarity in their
gait or fpeech, are fenfibly affected by it. For it is not only a very mortifying
fight, and a fight that ought not to be countenanced, for any man to fee his natural
infirmities fported with, but the audience do not fee him afterwards with the fame
pleafure. Thus it is doubly reprehenfible.

" STORACE too, fufpends, 'tis faid, her ftrains,

" If true---no lofs, while lovely LEAKE remains.

" Th' old girl, whenc'er fhe ftarts, 'tis *play and pay,*

" And as they could not pay, fhe would not play,

" Some think 'twas vaftly mean---but ' *that's her way.*'*

---

* We fear our author is here rather rafh and unjuft in his conclufion, as the anecdote annexed we think will prove; being at once a ftriking example of her *Roman virtue,* and *marked contempt of money.* A gentleman having fallen defperately in love with Signora Storace, (no accounting for people's tafte) found his heart in a fituation, which nothing but fleeping one night under the fame roof with her could poffibly alleviate. To accomplifh which, he had recourfe to a good-natured old foul, whom we have the *honor* to know, and from whom we had this, who taking pity on him, kindly undertook to wait upon Signora Storace, with an account of his malady, and a hundred pound bank note. which the good lady, with her rhetoric, had feldom found to fail. This fhe did immediately in Howland Street, where being introduced to Signora Storace, fhe briefly explained the object of her miffion, and prefented the reward of compliance. Storace, fhe faid, took the note in her hand, read it over, and faw that it was good. Afked her innumerable queftions, ftill holding, and now and then taking a wiftful peep at the Newland; as, " How any gentleman could think of fuch a thing? Who he was?" and fuch like. But at length all the Lucretia feizing her foul, fhe returned the note, and bade her old friend depart her lines. This we could not withhold from the world, as we have a great refpect for Signora Storace, and are therefore happy to refute the charges brought againft her of flinginefs.

" Next MOODY."

PASQUIN.

" What fomnific?"

WALDRON.

" As I hear,

" *Pair'd off* with Mother HOPKINS!"

PASQUIN.

" Precious pair!

" To make that fleepy mafs of av'rice* move,

" Does fure, O GRUBB! much in thy favour prove."

WALDRON.

" Ere now, by SHERRY, this good act was done,

" By fear made bold, he fent away the drone.†

---

* This heavy fon of Hibernia has acquired great riches by lending money to poor players, and fuch fort of folk. His affectionate regard for his wealth, has long fince rendered his name proverbial in the green room; fo that *a Moody*, and *a Mifer*, are there ufed as equivalent.

" Quid Avarus?
" Stultus et infanus."

The obfervations of Swift, " That we may fee how little God cares for riches, by the people he beftows them on," is well exemplified in Mr. Moody.

† Mr. M. was formerlydifcharged from old Drury, for endeavouring to *enforce*

L

PASQUIN.

" 'Twas well! But at this rate I have my fears,

" You foon will have more managefs than play'rs."

WALDRON.

" We've five!"

PASQUIN.

" One lefs, I never heard of more:"

WALDRON.

" The Duke* has join'd 'em, and commands the four.

the payment of five hundred pounds; a thing Mr. Sheridan *could not think of with any patience.* Previous to his difmiffion he wrote a vindictive letter to S. and exhibited it amongft his friends, threatening to read it publicly on the huftings at Stratford (the borough Sheridan reprefents) unlefs his demands were liquidated The town muft rejoice exceedingly at the feceffion of fuch an actor, as alfo the theatre, being as it is, thereby *unburthened* of him, the tax of nine pounds a week, and two hundred pounds a year, which he received for difgufting every audience he came before.

' The Duke of Clarence is faid to be a Robefpierre amongft thefe five Dictators, the will of the remainder depending on his nod. His Highnefs intends bringing out a farce of his own, in the courfe of the feafon, called the Manager in Diftrefs. The characters, from what we have feen of them, although they are taken from life, and poffefs fome wit, are, we think, upon the whole *very*

" All writers too, excepting one, you know!"

PASQUIN.

" Enough to ruin any houſe, I vow.

" Alas! poor Drury! what will now become on't?

" You all will ſtarve!"

WALDRON.

" Starve!!"

PASQUIN.

" Damme if you won't!

" Who'll go to fee what RICHARDSON* can write—

" Dull animal—or GRUBB† poor ſenſeleſs wight?

poor: how they are to *be caſt*, has not as yet tranſpired, but we do not ſuppoſe he will play in it himſelf."

* Richardſon wrote a *ſleepy*, inſipid play called the Fugitive. But what livelier ſtrain could be expected from a man who would rarely be awake two hours in the day, were it not for an indeſinent application of certain titillating corpuſcles to thoſe cavities that lead to the olfactory nerves, and which gently agitating the medulla of the brain, preclude all poſſible ſuſpenſion of the organs of ſenſe.

† The accompliſhed Mr. Grubb, lawyer, manager, and author of a *mournful* farce, entitled Alive and Merry, is alſo an actor, that is, he plays, where no one can prevent him, at his own theatre, Margate.

" Or CUMBERLAND,* with five act sermons boring

" Undisturb'd! unlefs 'tis with our snoring?

" Or who can sing-song, hodge-podge COBB,† endure;

" None, none, the barn will be deserted sure,

He treated his audience one night with himself in the character of Penrud-
dock, and to be sure he gave Mr. Cumberland's second edition of Shakspeare's
Timon, in a style peculiar to himself. We pronounce him a very original actor.
As a farce writer he is about a match for little Brewer, who has lately produced
a miserable one at the little theatre. If either of them depended upon his author-
ship for a subsistence, he would doubtless experience many woeful *Bannian days.*

* There is not a more envious man in existence than Mr. C. If you praise
another author in his company, he absolutely cannot sit upon his chair—he trem-
bles with envy. Yet he is a very good-natured man, and if you avoid that
particular chord, there is not a more entertaining companion. Applaud him! and
he from morn to night will lift and never tire. He has without doubt more merit
as a novelist, than as a writer of plays. Mr. C. would do well to recollect that
what might come with great propriety from the pulpit, is little less than dullness
on the stage.

" Omne tulit punctum, qui miscuit utile *dulci*,
" Lectorem *delectando*, pariterque monendo.
" Hic meret æra liber Sociis; hic & mare transit,
" Et longum noto scriptori prorogat ævum."

† We flatter ourselves with the idea that Mr. Cobb has concluded his career
with the death of Storace, and that we shall have no more patchwork from this
gentleman.

" And SHAW* on catgut fcrape his fharps and flats,

" To moral mice, and fentimental rats."

WALDRON.

" But SHERIDAN!"

PASQUIN.

" He write? Dick write? pfhaw! fluff!

" He knows too well that he has wrote enough."†

WALDRON.

" He will, he fays :"‡

PASQUIN.

" Words, words! 'tis all deception,

" I tell you, man, his Mufe is paft conception !§

---

* A violent Democrat, leader of the Drury-Lane band, and one of the Dictators of that Republic.

† Mr. Sheridan is one among the very few who have thought it wife, or had the power over themfelves, to caft anchor in the current of Succefs. He feized the critical moment, and while yet his Pegafus was found wind and limb, withdrew him from the race.

—————————Ne

Peccet ad extremum ridendus.　　HOR.

§ He has long held out this hope to the public, and has even received a fum for an opera, in which he declares he is far advanced, called The Caravan. " There are two bad pay mafters," fays the Proverb, " he who pays before hand, &c."--- Drury Lane feems to be both, for we do not believe he has written, or intends to write a line.

§ A late copy of verfes, compofed by Mr. S. on Capt. N. Ogle, who died in

M

" The jade gets old, a very ftumbler grown,

" Whom if he trufts, he lofes all he's won ;

" Bed-ridden quite, a faƈt, believe me, Sir,

" No bairns again he'll get—*at leaſt by her.*

" You've not a foul upon your books, I'm certain,

" Whofe works would pay for drawing up the curtain.

" Think you that St. JOHN, or that HOARE has wit?

" Haft feen his *Mahmoud,** read *St. Marguerite?*†

the Weft Indies, firmly perfuades us, that not only he will not attempt to write any more plays, but that he is not *now* able, however much he might defire it.---- We never witneffed more fcabrous lines, being exaƈtly, including their infipidity, what Ariftophanes calls, *profe on horfeback.* To infinuate, however, that Mr. Sheridan is not ftill a man of wit, is far from our intention, for we think he will yet give us an inftance of it, as would many other of our modern writers, by writing no more.

    We have long regarded him as a viƈtorious Δρομευς,
        ------who, crown'd with laurels, bravely won,
        Sits fmiling at the goal while others run.   YOUNG.

* Mahmoud, an opera recently produced by Mr. Hoare, fhews the vanity of authors. Becaufe Mr H. had been fuccefsful in two or three trifling farces, he afpired to the invention of an opera, in which he has plenarily expofed the weak-nefs of his mind. Stick to your laft !

† Mr. St. John wrote, befides this *opiatic* farce, a tragedy, which was nearly damned the firft night, although the houfe was filled with his friends. Charles Fox was prefent on this occafion, and exerted his utmoft to preferve it.

" Such forry dregs would prove we go and pay

" To fee fome favourite actor, not the play.

" And CUMBERLAND with truth muft e'en declare,

" He owes his beft fucceffes to the play'r.

" We can't but go, howe'er the piece be barren,

" If JORDAN's there, or *ftill* bewitching FARREN.*

" Or SUETT†, who by laughable grimace,

" Would fain oblivion give to PARSONS's face.

* Mifs Farren is an excellent actrefs. The fafcination of her fmile has been felt from peer to plebeian. But, alas! the time cannot be far diftant
When all thofe dimples fhall to wrinkles turn!
We fhould be happy if we could fay as much in favour of Mifs F's generofity as of her acting. She takes care of her mother, it is true, but this we think an act of but negative merit. Her benevolence is of a very confined nature; fo much fo that we incline to believe that fhe is alfo a *little bit* of a Jefuit. There is an article in their code, which runs thus: " Thofe Jefuits who fhew a greater *affection to their near relations* than to the fociety, are to be difcarded as enemies of the order—but fome other pretence muft be alledged for their expulfion."— This Mifs F. appears to have attended to with the greateft earneftnefs, having many poor relations and friends, who certainly do not enjoy a greater portion of her affection, than would become the ftricteft ftickler for Jefuitifm. There was a time when Mifs F. was not nurfed in the lap of eafe and plenty, and fhould, like Dido, as fhe is not ignorant of the frowns of fortune, have learnt to fuccour thofe who pine beneath their influence.
" Non ignara mali miferis, fuccurere difco."

† Suett would attempt to make us forget the inimitable Parfons, by furpaffing

· Or Bannister* with ſtir and endleſs rout,

" Whoſe fame will laſt---until he gets the gout!

" Shall Braham's notes mellifluent fill the void---

" Leake ſing and ſmile, and we not *be decoy'd?*

" Such ſounds exact the tribute of applauſe,

" Think not, O Hoare, thy doggrel is the cauſe.†

" 'Tis thus! now quickly ſay---aſſiſt my ſong,

" Which hence to Covent wings its way along---

his comic extravagance of features. This he can never do. To borrow a *grin* from the dead is however a venial fault. S. alſo copies, as well as he can, the departed Barret, in the part of Crazy, in Peeping Tom. Although greatly beholden to the *grave* for his *humour*, Mr. S. has, upon the whole, much merit. We only wiſh it was more original.

* It has ever appeared to us that Jack Banniſter is more indebted to his legs than to his head for the applauſe he obtains. Mr. Hoare's Prize was refuſed by Kemble as *unplayable* traſh, and was brought out by Signora Storace for her benefit, at the inſtigation of Mr. B. who, notwithſtanding its abſurdity, thought he could *kick it* into favour. Here he was ſucceſsful, but making a ſimilar effort in the Three and the Deuce, all his buſtle only ſerved to expedite its condemnation.

† The ſongs written by Hoare, O'Keefe, and Cobb, are paſſing-deſpicable. Yet we have no doubt that when either of theſe gentlemen hears them ſung, and applauded, he attributes it all to his verſes, if they may be ſo called, and never to the voice of the ſinger, or the taſte of the compoſer.

" What's left unfung!"

WALDRON.

" CROUCH, KELLY, yet remain,

" Young KEMBLE, SIDDONS, MILLER, and a train

" Moft numerous!"

PASQUIN.

" Ah! CROUCH! thy day is o'er,

" ' Cold is that breaft, which warm'd the world before,'*

" Thy †*Irifh nightingale* now roves, I fear,

" And heedlefs quits ' *his loaf, his only tear*."

* Mrs. Crouch, the once beautiful and admired Crouch, is now haftily lofing all her attraction. It will not furprife any one much to be told that fhe is *a perfect ftranger to this;* but it muft make many fmile to hear that fhe is at the prefent moment learning from Monfieur ———— *to fing a note lower.*

† The *cognomen* of *Irifh nightingale*, has long been enjoyed by Mr. Kelly. As a finger he is juft the reverfe of Incledon. K's voice is neither capacious nor melodius; Incledon's is both : the firft poffeffes much fcience, the latter is rude and uncultivated. As actors, I will not pretend to adjudge the palm! Mr. K. has, to be fure, a certain fomething in his voice highly captivating to female ears, and which is vilely termed a brogue. This is not now fo evident as when he firft made his appearance on the London boards. It has oft diverted us to liften to him, when finging thefe two lines, with his peculiar pronunciation.

" Sure thou wert born to pleafe me,
" My love, my only dear."

N

" Faſt SIDDONS wains! Young KEMBLE* needs not wait ⎤

" For time to ſilver o'er his gloomy pate, ⎬

" But with my free conſent, and WATHEN,† beat retreat. ⎦

" MILLER has powers, is young, and will improve,

" And if ſhe ſings not, win upon our love.

He lately attempted an Iriſh character in Hooke's childiſh opera, and here, like Macready in ſuch perſonations, we never heard him ſpeak *Engliſh with more propriety and clearneſs.*

Mr. K's flame for his " only *tear,*" is certainly greatly abated, ſince he now wanders about in the capacity of a ſinging maſter, leaving " his *loaf,*" under the care of an unfortunate *half-ſtarved Frenchman.*

* Young Kemble will never make a player. The character he plays the beſt is *Vapour*—he is here, to be ſure, inimitable, in the effect he gives it—Who can ſee him without having the vapours ? The pride of this family would be ſurpriſing, were it not ſo common to thoſe who riſe from a low origin. We remember, a few years ſince, meeting this young man with a ſtick over his ſhoulder, on which was a bundle, walking unabaſhed through the public ſtreets. He is now, without merit to apologize for it, as proud as any of his relations, and

" Forgets the little plough-boy, that whiſtled o'er the lee."

Young Palmer alſo does not promiſe to make any great figure. His counte- nance is good ; but, as the fox ſaid of the vizor, " What a pity 'tis it has got no brains."

† The Captain might do very well as a player among Lords, but the Lord deliver us from ſeeing him play amongſt actors.

" Now Covent Garden come before my view !"

WALDRON.

" Then I depart---farewel !"

PASQUIN.

" Adieu, adieu!

" HARRIS appear, and bring thy ragamuffin crew.*

" No bring them not---too oft already they

" Have been the *heavy burthen* of our lay.

" LEWIS declines---when dreffed, with eyes afkew,

" He imitates no buck, except old Q.

" His time's gone by, he ftuffs falfe calves in vain,

" For ftill the *ancient calf* is feen too plain.

---

* Mr. Harris has, undoubtedly, to do with a pack of *keen dogs*. If he neg-
lected to pay them one week, he'd have the whole kennel to range in by himfelf
the next. Having been bred a coach-maker, or fome fuch elegant trade, he
knows how neceffary it is to be ready with the ftuff on the Saturday night, and thus
prevents all thoughts of defertion. His former occupation may alfo be fairly fup-
pofed to influence his mind in his felections for the theatre. His writers, actors,
and the manner in which he gets up pieces, fhew very plainly what a refined genius he poffeffes. He lives at Uxbridge, where he keeps a congenial foul of the
feminine gender, with whom he fots unaccountably.

"*Holman has voice; I grant 'tis ſtrong and good---

" But why for ever think he's in a wood?

" Then crying WALLIS† ne'er with POPE ſhall vie,

" Whate'er her friends avouch, or papers lie---

" Which you may think your intereſt to buy.

    * The continual rant and roar of Mr. Holman proceeds from his want of judgment. The impreſſion he made at his firſt appearance gradually wears away. He becomes corpulent, his ſhoulders are high and ungraceful, yet he, like every other ſtage-ſtruck hero, thinks himſelf a Garrick. Alas! we promiſe fair to ſee no more Garricks.

        " Natura il fece e poi ruppe la ſtampa."
                              ARIOSTO.

    Many are very prompt to fancy that actors, from what they ſee of them on the ſtage, muſt neceſſarily be the moſt amuſing companions in private ; but they are greatly miſtaken. " The learning *pages by heart*," ſays Locke, in his Thoughts on Education, " no more fits the memory for retention of *any thing elſe*, than the graving of one ſentence *in lead*, makes it the more capable of retaining firmly any other characters. If ſuch a ſort of exerciſe of the memory were able to give it ſtrength, and improve our parts, *players*, of all other people, muſt needs have the beſt memories, and be beſt company. But whether *the ſcraps they have got in their heads* this way, make them remember other things the better, and whether their parts be improved proportionably to the pains they have taken in getting by heart others ſayings, *experience will ſhew*." This we do not notice as applying more to Mr. H. than to the whole body-dramatic ; and to correct, at the ſame time, the ungrounded notion ſome people entertain of them.

    † Miſs Wallis's form and face poſſeſs much prettyneſs, but ſhe always ſeems

" Too deep fhe play'd---you, fapient, made a catch,

" (For greateft rogues will fometimes meet their match)

" Engag'd her faft---paid dearly for your treafure,

" And now repent your folly at your leifure.

" Good MATTOCKS, '*fhe's done up,*' fhe is; 'tis faĉt,

" And will *be difh'd* if fhe perfift to aĉt.

" And MARTYR too, in faith does not grow younger,

" And QUICK, ah! well a day, can't fqueak much longer.

" The reft!---in pity PASQUIN names them not---

" Sure HARRIS you muft thank him they're forgot!*

" 'Tis faid you pay---'tis truth, per force, 'tis truth,

" For all your vagrants live from hand to mouth.†

to weep or to have been weeping—her voice is monotonous, and incapable of giving any great effeĉt to the fpeeches fhe has to deliver in the feveral charaĉters from Shakfpeare, which fhe has attempted. Harris, *he* is forry to fay, has her for three years certain, at fixteen pounds a week.

* As a tragedian, Mr. Harley often pleafed, and never difgufted us. But Mr. Harris, unwilling that any aĉtor fhould be better than another, or wifer than the manager himfelf, has difmiffed him. Surely no houfe in all its departments could ever vaunt of more confiftency than Covent Garden!

† Mr. Powell of Covent Garden theatre is an exception to this general rule; for he, fo far from labouring under any fuch emergency, often afks his needy

O

" In actors Drury highly bears the belle---

" In authors which---I leave for heav'n to tell!*

" Should honeſt REYNOLDS† once his force withdraw,

" You've ſcarce a writer left, that's worth a ſtraw.

brethren to dinner. The ſingular manner in which he treats his viſitors may create a ſmile. Mr. P. never gives even a beef ſteak or a mutton chop to them, which is not dreſſed by a man cook. This *character he performs himſelf* to admiration ; ſtanding over the fire in the room where they dine, frying and broiling away, until his friends *are all quite perfect in their parts,* and can eat no more. He then takes the poker, which he had prepared, red hot from the fire, and addreſſes his company in theſe few, but very expreſſive words, " Don't you think you'd better go ?" To which they, knowing his humour, always reply, " Yes, certainly, Mr. Powell, *if you think ſo,*" and exeunt. If they do not, he immediately proceeds to action, and drives them out per force, for he will not permit them to ſit a moment after they have done eating. He takes his motto from Horace.

" ——Ediſti ſatis atque bibiſti :
" Tempus abire tibi."

* Non noſtrum inter vos tantas componere lites! VIRG.

Old Macklin being aſked his opinion of the ſtage in its preſent ſtate, replied in theſe lines, which, conſidering his years, are very neat, and ſmack ſtrongly of the ſarcaſtic humour of the veteran in his juvenile days.

" Thus ſtands the ſtage—new Drury cannot pay, ⎫
" And Covent's actors if they're paid, muſt ſay ⎬
" They don't deſerve it, for they cannot play." ⎭

† The many amiable qualities of Mr. Reynolds hold him in great eſteem with

" O'Keefe,* poor fellow ! fometimes may fuccced---

" May make us fmile---but *ne'er can make us read!*

" His plays are fields with poppies rich abounding,

" Where every thing but common-fenfe is found-in :

" To Robinson's† fine hi, te, ti, te, ti !

" This obfervation alfo may apply.

all who know him. As a writer he is infinitely the beft of thofe who mean to contribute to the amufement of Covent Garden. He has already, we hope, over-come the *literary indifpofition,* which always attends him upon the winding up of his plays, and placed his annual tribute in the hands of Mr. Harris ; from whofe *mauling paws,* whenever it iffues, we are fure it will be *a further addition to the few refpectable productions of the modern ftage.*

    * The works of Mr. O'Keefe are in general fo exceedingly outré, fo extrava-gantly whimfical, that one cannot well fee them without a fmile. To read them is a thing utterly impracticable. We think, from the Magic Banner, that we have not much more to expect from him. It was impoffible for us to fee that play with-out exclaiming, " Alas! poor O'Keefe ! where be your gibes now? your gambols? your fongs ? your flafhes of merriment, that were wont to fet the *galleries* in a roar? Not one now !"

    † Lord Shaftfbury fays, the *fenfus communis,* is a fenfe very feldom found among the great. We believe it ; and therefore Mrs. Robinfon's poems are feen in the windows of many people of fafhion. We like fomething more than words in poetic compofitions : no one will find any thing elfe in Mrs. R's. *Verfus inopes rerum nugæque canoræ.* The works of women who inhabit the regions of fafhion, from their price, may be well compared to filver, in the purchafe of which, the *fafhion* is always rated at ten times, at leaft, the intrinfic value of the thing itfelf.

" With lofty tip-top inane phrafes beaming,

" And metaphors and figures wond'rous, teeming,

" On vellum printed, and *but* charg'd a guinea,

" Vancenza's in the hand of---ev'ry ninny!

" Anxious they read! and read!! it is fo clever!!

" Then rife, and find themfelves---as wife as ever.

" Prize REYNOLDS' humour for it fuits the town.

" 'Tis good, original, and all his own.

" No pilf'rer he---whate'er he fays he writ,

" He writ! he never borrows other's wit :

" Would fcorn an act that's mean, and blufh'd to fee

" His empty friend tax'd home with roguery.

" Alas! poor MORTON! of Zorinfkian fame,

" How have you toil'd, and well deferv'd---your fhame.

" None's fafe with you, for lately, wanting prey,

" You took e'en REYNOLDS' characters away.

" And now, could he retaliation chufe,

" You know full well you *have not one* to lofe.

" Thus indifcriminate, ' *alive or dead*,'

" You fteal from all, and ' *grind and make your bread.*'

" But hark ye there, who labour with the fpleen---
" Haft feen Tom's picture in the magazine?
" Doft think he did not pay to have it in?
" His life too---hold your laughter if you can---
" ' Ohe jam fatis eft' of fuch a man.*

* It is very generally known that there is nothing more common to editors of magazines than to receive five or ten guineas, according to their circulation, for permitting the head of any would-be author, or egregious coxcomb, to appear in the work, with fome hyperbolical account of his wonderful good qualities, miraculous genius, and confequently unheard-of perfecution. In this cafe there can be no doubt of the fact. Mr. Morton, to gratify a contemptible vanity, and to attempt to refute charges he never could even meet his friends upon without confufion, has availed himfelf of a trumpery publication, now offering itfelf to any one at a very trifling rate, in which he has given an engraving of his *fweet face*; procuring fome one of the fcribes, the beft of whom would rejoice to do it for half a guinea, to write, as a biographical fketch, whatever Mr. M. could invent in his own favour to accompany it. We however being acquainted with this gentleman's literary as well as private character, fhall in a few lines give the former to our readers, left by any accident the Monthly Mirror fhould fall into their hands, of which there is no great fear, and lead them into a falfe conclufion on the juftice of his claims to the approbation of the world.

The infipid writer of this biographical fketch, as it is called, of *Squire Morton*, commences by ftating, that " the object of that department is to communicate facts; we fhall content ourfelves with telling the truth, a pleafure his venality obliged him to overlook.

Mr. Morton, nephew to Maddifon the lottery office keeper, near Charing-Crofs, was educated at a fchool in Soho; where he is remembered more for having idled away his time with Holman, in fpouting plays, than for indulging a laudable emulation to excel his fchool-fellows. They foon left this feminary together, and were intended by their friends to follow *refpectable* profeffions, but *deftiny* whofe *decree is irreverfible*, had doomed Morton to *make* plays, and Holman to act them.

As a writer Mr. M. has not been without his fhare of abufe; perhaps he has *not* had more than his fhare. His firft production was Columbus, which though bad in the extreme, was claimed and clearly proved, by Mr. Thelwall, to have been written by him, and by clandeftine means nearly copied by Mr. M. It is alledged, by way of apology for the latter, that no two writers can take a plot from Marmontel without introducing the fame characters, incidents and fentiments, and making their pieces undeftinguifhably identick. We cannot for a moment allow the truth of a pofition fo puerile and ridiculous. And we fear fuch a marvellous coincidence of mental operation, will meet with but little credit, where Mr. M. is a party concerned. He next came forward with the Children in the Wood, which he did not think proper to acknowledge, we may reafonably fuppofe, until he was pretty well affured that his mutilations, from no claimants appearing, had baffled all difcovery.

" Thus bad begins, but worfe remains behind."

He then produced Zorinfki, to make up which he had metamorphofed and mangled Brooke's Guftavus Vafa, one of the fineft written plays in our language. This plagiary might have long remained a fecret, but for the ingenious refearch of an anonymous writer, under the fignature of Truth, who was evidently actuated by no other motive than to expofe impudent audacity and fhamelefs impofture. Thefe ftrictures firft made their appearance in a morning paper, and were afterwards collected together, and publifhed in a pamphlet. The language is nervous and energetic; the writer boldly advances what he firmly eftablifhes.— He does not, as is ufual with men actuated by bafe motives, affert without proof, or accufe without teftimony, but with the utmoft candour and plainnefs, brings forward whole fpeeches from Guftavus, copied literally by Morton in his Zorinfki.

The different thefts thus proved, we do not fee what it can avail in his favour that we fhould be told that Brooke's play is as notorious, and as well known as any of Shakfpeare's, and that a man would be as fafe from detection in taking from the one as the other. For granting this to be the truth in the prefent inftance, it only goes to fhew Mr. M. to be a more audacious plunderer than he would otherwife appear.

Attacked in this formidable manner, he knew not how to act; he dared not deny the charge, and his fear pronounced him guilty.

'Ίνα γὰρ δέ(3᾽, ἵνα καὶ αἰδώς. Luc.

The manager, neverthelefs, profited greatly by this champion of Truth; and to him may certainly be afcribed the immenfe influx of cafh into the treafury, and not to the merits of Zorinfki, for Mr. M. had made fuch wretched ufe of the foreign aid he had borrowed, and intermixed with it fo much of his *own* wit, as to render it *miferabile vifu!* An attempt was made to give *it a run* at Covent Garden, but having to depend on its own merit, for full benches, and no longer on the voice of accufation—it was played one night, to an empty houfe.

He is faid in his life, " to poffefs that happy art of felecting from the ftores of half-forgotten ballads, &c. &c." *we think this was a confeffion perfectly unneceffary.*

Carmina Morton emit: recitat fua carmina Morton :
Nam quod emis, poffis dicere jure tuum. Mart.

We are then informed that, with all thefe blufhing honours on his head, he had the nerves " To go his three nights to the treafury—whiftle an opera tune—put the receipts in his pockets—and to think about *manufacturing* another play." Thus is Mr. M. depicted, like the evil angel in Addifon's Campaign,

" Smiling in the tumult and enjoying the ftorm ;"

that is, hugging himfelf in the fuccefs of his own craft, laughing at the public infatuation, and pocketing up their pence?"

" Not fo with ANDREWS,* humble plodding cit—
" As genuine in his women as in his wit.

His laft effort, brought out at Covent Garden laft feafon, is a lame imitation of Reynolds's originality. Every character, and the greater part of the incidents, are taken from Mr. R's Notoriety, Dramatift, Rage, &c. &c. *O imitatores servum pecus!* The refemblance alfo is fo great to Speculation, that many people are of opinion, that Mr. R. finding he had much more to fay for each of his characters than he could introduce, gave it to his friend Morton, and helped him to work it up into the Way to get Married; and Frederick for the prefent good-naturedly lets him enjoy the credit of it.

If it be fair to judge of the future by the paft, we may form a tolerable idea of what we have to expect from Mr. Morton. The greateft misfortune for him is, that genius is not an acquifition, and as he is now returned from the Ifle of Wight, where he has been making *his felections in his ufual ftyle* for another play, we would advife him, for the fake of the remnant of his reputation as an author, to adopt the honefty of Terence, and to infert fomething equivalent to the two fubfequent verfes in the prologue to all his future *compofitions.*

> Quæ convenere, in Adriam ex Perinthia
> Fatetur tranftuliffe, atque ufum pro fuis.

M. P. Andrews, M. P. the redoubted member for Bewdley, is a very fingular man, both in his writings and his amours. His pieces are purely original. His *grey nymph*, whofe flowing ringlets entwine his little doating heart, in rapturous *blind* delight, is an unique. Her ftyle of playing in private, tickled the member's fancy fo much, that he recommended her to the manager of Covent Garden to perform Mifs Wallis's *comic* character in the Myfteries of the Caftle. This was not agreed to by Harris. She is, however, we underftand engaged by

" He takes from none---no keen-eyed book-worm fears,

" As in his *Myſt'ries* clearly it appears.

" Who can, who dares of plagiary indite it---

" I ſwear that he, and only he could write it!

" O! ANDREWS! reſt aſſur'd, the fates deſign

" No one ſhall *envy* any *piece* of thine.

" HOLCROFT, quite ſapleſs grown, can write no more---

" His body's feeble, and his mind is poor.*

Colman to fit as My Grandmother, inſtead of the picture in the farce of that title. As the trick is too palpable in the tranſition from the canvas to Miſs Leake, we think the effect will be heightened. The *divine object* of our contemplation is admirably deſcribed in theſe four lines.

" Quel âge a *cette Iris,* dont on fait tant de bruit ?
" Me demandoit Cliton n'aguerre.
" Il faut, dis je, vous fatisfaire,
" Elle a *vingt ans le jour,* et *ſoixante ans la nuit.*"

How *mature,* how *ripe,* and perfect, muſt be the joys ariſing from an inter-courſe of ſouls, with one whom *time* has rendered *dexterouſly* ſkilful in all the ideal or theoretical, and practical blandiſhments of love! O happy, thrice happy, Peter!

* Mr. Holcroft's great tenet for a long time was, that the mind is ſo com-pletely independent on the material part of man, that it cannot be effected by any diſeaſe incident to the human frame.

" Nor rolling ſeas, nor an impetuous wind,
" Can overſet the ballaſt of the mind." WALKER'S EPICTETUS.

Q

" Had TOPHAM genius, and the fame it gives,

" (The *world* well knows no greater blockhead lives)

" I could not praife him, for my foul abhors

" The man who breaks through Nature's fweeteft laws---

" Whofe heart fo callous to each tender tie,

" So deaf to gratitude---to pity's figh---

" Can fee that form he vilely has betray'd,

" Now pine in want, and never lend his aid.

" Alas! much injur'd, beauteous, gen'rous WELLS,

" How oft on thee my thought with forrow dwells.

" Accept a tear---'tis all I can beftow---

" That, and to hate the author of thy woe.*

Mr. H. however, has furvived his opinion, and is himfelf a proof of its fallacioufnefs. His mind is much debilitated by the various fhocks his body has fuftained, and he can now ferve for little elfe, but to ftand in the crofs road of Faction, and point out to his fellow-citizens—THE ROAD TO RUIN.

* The ingratitude of Mr. Topham to poor Wells, muft receive the marked deteftation of every honeft man. After living upon her falary, and exhaufting her finances, even to the laft farthing, he deferted her to want and mifery in the King's Bench—a living inftance of female affection betrayed and infulted. By him the town is deprived of the excellent powers of Mrs. Wells on the ftage, than whom a more engaging actrefs never graced its boards; and fhe, whofe generous hand, when

" Enough, enough!　My Thefpian fong is done---

" The herd difmifs'd !---and is there living one,

" Who thinks I do not all their worth allow them---

" Believe me, 'tis---becaufe he docs *not know them*."

competent, was to the *indigent world*, in its bounty, as univerfal as the fun, who never rofe but to pity and relieve, is now fo much reduced as to need others charity and commiferation.

☞ We cannot refrain from making two or three obfervations on the preceding fatire, whereby we would prove that our author is entitled to every eftimation as a fatirift.　" *Dictio fatira*," fays Voffius, " *laudatur non tam poetica, quam pedeftris, ac fermoni fimilis, peneque extemporalis*."　That he has obferved this rule, as well as that of *abrupta omnia*, with fome few exceptions, we think *no one* will fcruple to acknowledge.　They will, therefore, inevitably allow him great praife; fince an adherence to thefe precepts is well known to be perfectly in the ftyle of Horace. And to thofe who, overflowing with tendernefs, may affirm " that fatire ought rather to touch on thofe vices of men which it might ridicule, than thofe which it fhould reprove ferioufly;" and thence, on account of fome harfh paffage, take occafion of condemning our poet, we reply in the words of Trapp, in his *Prælectiones poetica*, to a like objection :—*Quod fi verum eft, inter vates fatiricos Juvenalis vix erit numerandus.　Quanquam enim interdum ridet, plerumque ferio agit; rarius jocis plerumque flagello, utitur*.　And we fhall even be contented if fuch a difference of opinion fhould induce a few to rank *him no higher* than Juvenal.

Virgil, Horace, Ovid, and various other poets, have affured themfelves, in their writings, of immortality; whether with *more title than our bard*, fome people will not think *very doubtful;* but judging from what has been advanced, and from Fontenelle's maxim, that " thofe who would write for immortality, fhould write about fools," his brows appear to us already encircled with the envied wreath :—

And surely he might, were the late Lord Barrymore living, with truth ejaculate:

> " Non ego pauperum
> " Sanguis parentum, non ego, (quem vocant)
> " Dilecte Mæcenas, obibo,
> " Nec Stygiâ cohibebor undâ.

FINIS.